WHY DO ANIMALS LOOK LIKE THAT?

Sam George

Educational Media

rourkeeducationalmedia.com

Scan for Related Titles
and Teacher Resources

Teaching Focus:

Concepts of Print: Ending Punctuation- Have students locate the ending punctuation for sentences in the book. Count how many times a period, question mark, or exclamation point is used. Which one is used the most? What is the purpose for each ending punctuation mark? Practice reading these sentences with appropriate expression.

Before Reading:

Building Academic Vocabulary and Background Knowledge

Before reading a book, it is important to set the stage for your child or student by using pre-reading strategies. This will help them develop their vocabulary, increase their reading comprehension, and make connections across the curriculum.

1. Read the title and look at the cover. *Let's make predictions about what this book will be about.*
2. Take a picture walk by talking about the pictures/photographs in the book. Implant the vocabulary as you take the picture walk. Be sure to talk about the text features such as headings, Table of Contents, glossary, bolded words, captions, charts/diagrams, and Index.
3. Have students read the first page of text with you then have students read the remaining text.
4. Strategy Talk – use to assist students while reading.
    - Get your mouth ready
    - Look at the picture
    - Think…does it make sense
    - Think…does it look right
    - Think…does it sound right
    - Chunk it – by looking for a part you know
5. Read it again.
6. After reading the book complete the activities below.

Content Area Vocabulary
Use glossary words in a sentence.

camouflage
habitat
independent
prey
snouts
treks

After Reading:

Comprehension and Extension Activity

After reading the book, work on the following questions with your child or students in order to check their level of reading comprehension and content mastery.

1. *Why do you think the food a flamingo eats changes the color of its feathers?* (Summarize)
2. *What is a marsupial? Can you name two?* (Asking questions)
3. *What is the purpose of the hump on a camel's back?* (Text to self connection)
4. *Why are tusks important to walruses survival?* (Asking questions)

Extension Activity

There are many reasons animals look the way they do. They have to adapt to their surroundings to stay safe from predators and the climates they live in. Using a piece of poster board, make a chart of the animals discussed in the book. List the animal name at the top and the different things each one does to stay safe or adapt to their habitat underneath each animal. Do any of them have things in common? What were they?

Table of Contents

Habitats

Animals look the way they do for a reason. Most often, the reason is related to an animal's survival and **habitat**.

Many monkeys have long tails
to help them climb trees.
Their tails also help them swing from
branch to branch, and tree to tree.

Polar bears live in a cold and icy habitat. They live on the sea ice of the Arctic Circle, by the North Pole.

Their white fur keeps them warm. It also blends in with their icy habitat to help them hunt seals, their favorite food.

Walruses are also found in the Arctic Circle. They have long front teeth called tusks. Tusks are important to walruses' survival. They rely on them to drag their huge bodies out of the icy water.

 If trapped under ice, walruses use their tusks to make holes in it so they can breathe.

Marsupials

Kangaroos and koala bears are marsupials, animals that carry their babies in pouches. Marsupial babies are called joeys.

Carrying joeys in pouches makes hopping easier for female kangaroos, and climbing easier for koala bears. A joey stays in its mama's pouch until it is old enough to be **independent.**

Food and Color

Alligators and anteaters have long **snouts**. Anteaters dig with their claws to find ants and termites to eat. They put their snout in the hole and use their long tongues to slurp up bugs.

Alligators' strong, broad jaws are useful for cracking the shells of turtles and other hard-shelled **prey.**

Anteaters have no teeth. Alligators have lots!

Flamingos are born with gray feathers. Their color changes when they begin eating shrimp and algae. The food they eat turns their feathers pink.

Beating the Heat

Camels have humps on their backs. They store fat in them so they will not need to eat during long **treks** through the hot desert.

 As camels use their stored energy, their humps grow smaller. When they eat and drink, their humps grow big again.

Flap. Flap. Flap.

The African elephants' ears are flapping. Its habitat is very hot. Flapping their big ears like fans helps keep them cool.

Elephants also live in Asia. Asian elephants have smaller ears. Can you think why that might be?

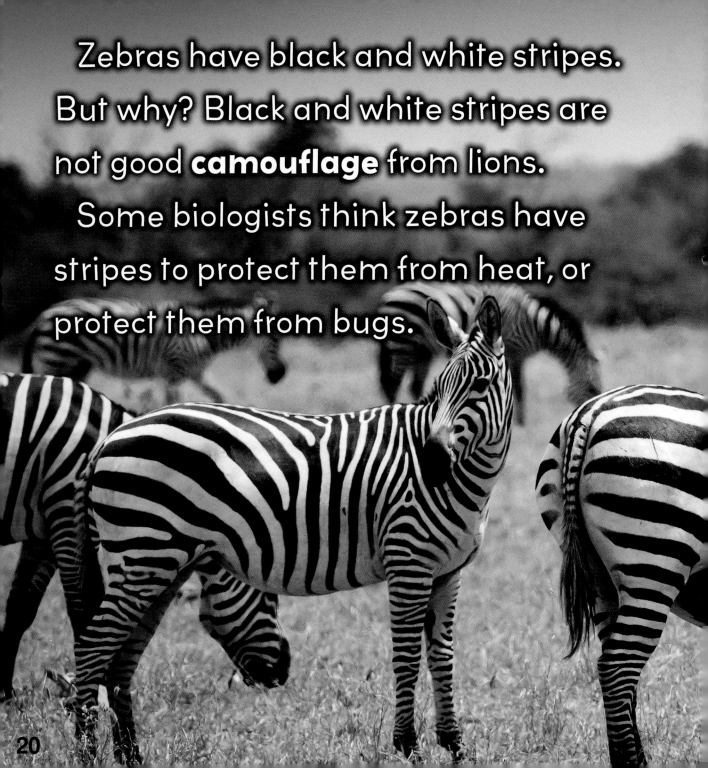

Zebras have black and white stripes. But why? Black and white stripes are not good **camouflage** from lions.

Some biologists think zebras have stripes to protect them from heat, or protect them from bugs.

Biologists have ideas about why zebras have stripes, but more study is needed. Perhaps you will be a biologist and solve the riddle!

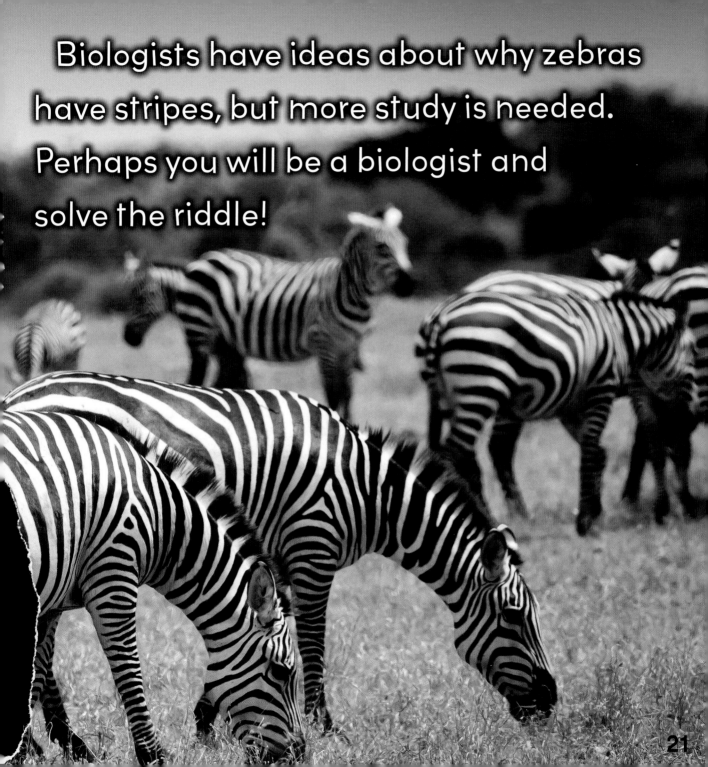

Photo Glossary

camouflage (KAM-uh-flahzh): Coloring or covering that makes animals, people, and objects look like their surroundings.

habitat (HAB-uh-tat): The place and natural conditions in which a plant or an animal lives.

independent (in-di-PEN-duhn If an animal or person is independent, they do not need or want much help or assistan